RAINBOW
magic ®

The Pet Keeper Fairies

For Lauren Mary Shepherd,
my beautiful niece

Special thanks to
Narinder Dhami

ORCHARD BOOKS
338 Euston Road, London NW1 3BH
Orchard Books Australia
Hachette Children's Books
Level 17/207 Kent Street, Sydney, NSW 2000
A Paperback Original
First published in Great Britain in 2006
Rainbow Magic is a registered trademark of Working Partners Limited.
Series created by Working Partners Limited, London W6 OQT
Text © Working Partners Limited 2006
Illustrations © Georgie Ripper 2006
The right of Georgie Ripper to be identified as the illustrator
of this work has been asserted by her in accordance
with the Copyright, Designs and Patents Act, 1988.
A CIP catalogue record for this book is available
from the British Library.
ISBN 1 84616 169 X
1 3 5 7 9 10 8 6 4 2

Printed and bound in China

Lauren the Puppy Fairy

by Daisy Meadows

illustrated by Georgie Ripper

ORCHARD BOOKS

www.rainbowmagic.co.uk

The Fairyland Palace

Wetherbury Village

Strawberry Farm

The Spring Show

Fairies with their pets I see
And yet no pet has chosen me!
So I will get some of my own
To share my perfect frosty home.

This spell I cast. Its aim is clear:
To bring the magic pets straight here.
Pet Keeper Fairies soon will see
Their seven pets living with me!

Contents

Puppies on Show

"Look at that marrow, Kirsty," Rachel Walker laughed, pointing at the large green vegetable on the display table. "It's nearly as big as I am!"

Kirsty Tate read the card propped against the marrow. "It's won a prize," she announced, "for Biggest Vegetable at the Wetherbury Spring Show."

There were other enormous vegetables on the table too, and the girls stared at the giant-sized carrots and onions. There were also huge bowls of daffodils, tulips and bluebells. The best flower displays had won prizes too.

"This is great!" Rachel declared, as she finished her candyfloss. "I wish we had a Spring Show back home."

Rachel was staying in Wetherbury with Kirsty for the Easter holidays, and the girls had spent the whole afternoon at the show. The field was crammed with stalls selling home-made cakes, biscuits and jams, and there was a tombola, a hoopla and a coconut shy, as well as pony rides and a huge red and yellow bouncy castle. Rachel and Kirsty had really enjoyed themselves.

"I think we've been round the whole show," Kirsty said at last. "Mum and Dad will be here to pick us up soon."

"Shall we have one last look at our favourite stall?" asked Rachel eagerly.

"You mean the one for Wetherbury Animal Shelter?" Kirsty said with a smile.

Rachel nodded. "I want to see if they've found homes for those four puppies."

"I hope so," Kirsty said. "They were really cute! And talking of pets…" She lowered her voice so that she wouldn't be overheard. "Do you think we might find another fairy pet today?"

"We'll just have to keep our eyes open!" Rachel whispered in a determined voice.

No one else knew Kirsty and Rachel's wonderful secret. They were friends with the fairies, and whenever there was trouble in Fairyland, the girls were always happy to help. Cold, spiteful Jack Frost was often causing problems for the fairies, and now he had stolen the magical animals belonging to the seven Pet Keeper Fairies! But the mischievous pets had escaped from Jack Frost into the human world. Rachel and Kirsty were trying to find the pets and return them to their fairy owners, before Jack Frost's goblin servants caught them and took them back to their master's ice castle.

"It's a pity Jack Frost can't get his own pet, instead of trying to steal someone else's!" Kirsty remarked.

"Yes, but remember what the fairies told us," Rachel reminded her. "In Fairyland, the pets choose their owners – and none of them has ever chosen Jack Frost!"

"There must be the perfect pet for him somewhere," Kirsty said thoughtfully. "But it would have to be quite mean, just like him!"

The girls headed towards the animal shelter stall. But as they got nearer, Rachel's face fell. "Look, Kirsty," she said sadly. "There's one puppy left."

Next to the stall was a large pen.

When the girls had been there a few
hours earlier, there had been four
puppies in it, one brown, one white,
and two black and
white ones. Now
only one black and
white pup remained.
He was sitting in
a corner, chewing
on a piece of rope.

"Oh, what a shame,"
Kirsty sighed. She bent
over the pen and the puppy
immediately dropped the rope and
bounced over to be stroked, his tail
wagging furiously. "He looks lonely."

Mr Gregory, the vet who ran the
animal shelter, was taking down the
posters that were pinned up on the stall.

15

Kirsty smiled at him. She'd taken her kitten, Pearl, to Mr Gregory's surgery in Wetherbury for her injections.

"Hello," Mr Gregory said, smiling back. "It's Kirsty Tate, isn't it? How's Pearl?"

Kirsty grinned. "She's gorgeous!" she replied. "What's the puppy called, Mr Gregory?"

"I call him Bouncer," the vet replied, "but it'll be up to his new owners to give him his proper name."

The puppy was licking Kirsty's fingers through the wire netting. He looked so adorable with his head on one side that the girls just couldn't understand why no one had given him a home yet.

"Do you need any help to pack up?" Rachel asked Mr Gregory, as he began clearing leaflets from the table.

"That's very kind of you," Mr Gregory said gratefully. "Would you mind taking Bouncer for a quick walk round the showground? He's been cooped up in the pen all day."

Rachel and Kirsty looked at each other in delight. "We'd love to!" they chorused.

Mr Gregory took a lead from his pocket and opened the pen. The puppy looked very excited when he saw the lead. He bounced around, giving little yaps of joy as the vet attached the lead to the pup's collar. "You walk him first," Rachel said to Kirsty. Kirsty took the lead and they set off, the puppy running along beside them.

"Don't be too long, girls," Mr Gregory called. "It'll only take me half an hour to pack up."

"OK," Rachel replied with a wave.

The puppy pulled excitedly at the lead, sniffing here and there, as the girls walked between the stalls. Everyone else was starting to pack up too. There were still a few children left on the bouncy castle, but their parents were doing their best to remove them from it so that it could be deflated.

"I think Bouncer's going to pull my arm off!" Kirsty laughed as the puppy strained to go faster. "He's so excited."

"That's because he's just spotted another dog," Rachel said, pointing ahead.

A brown and white puppy with a shaggy coat and long, floppy ears had seen them too, and he came bounding down the hill towards them.

"Isn't he lovely?" Kirsty laughed, as the pup drew nearer, waving his tail in greeting. "He's a springer spaniel, I think."

Bouncer was dancing around the girls' legs, obviously bursting with excitement at the sight of his new friend. The spaniel ran up to them, gave a little yap and dashed off.

Bouncer hurtled after him and both girls' eyes widened in horror as they realised that the lead was now hanging loosely in Kirsty's hand. Somehow, Bouncer had got free!

"Oh, no!" Rachel gasped. "How did that happen?"

"I don't know," Kirsty replied, anxiously. "But we'd better get him back right away!"

Puppy, Come Back!

Quickly Rachel and Kirsty ran after the excited puppy.

"I'm sure the lead was fixed to Bouncer's collar properly, Rachel," Kirsty panted. "There's something very strange going on here."

"You could be right," Rachel agreed, as she caught up with the puppies.

The two dogs had stopped chasing each other, and were now running round in circles, snapping playfully at each other's tails.

Kirsty looked round. "At least they're quite safe here," she pointed out. The puppies were in a corner of the showground, not far from the high fence which separated the field from the road. "They can't get out onto the road."

"I wonder where the spaniel's owner is?" Rachel said, sounding worried. "I can't see anyone about."

"I think there's a name tag on his collar," Kirsty said. She bent over the two puppies, who were rolling about on the grass. "Look, Rachel."

The girls stared closely at the spaniel's blue collar. A name tag in the shape of a little silver bone hung from it, and "Sunny" was written there in glittering blue letters.

"Hello, Sunny," said Kirsty.

The spaniel licked Kirsty's hand, staring up at her with big brown eyes.

"There's no phone number or address," Rachel said, taking a closer look at the name tag.

"Let's tell Mr Gregory when we take Bouncer back," Kirsty suggested. "He'll know what to do."

"Good idea," agreed Rachel.

Tail wagging, Sunny jumped to his feet and gave a happy little yap. Next moment, to Rachel and Kirsty's amazement, a sparkly, red rubber ball appeared in mid-air and fell to the ground! The spaniel pounced on it and then nudged it towards Bouncer.

"Did you see that, Kirsty?" Rachel gasped. "Or did I imagine it?"

"I saw a ball appear from thin air, if that's what you mean!" Kirsty replied, her voice shaking with excitement. The two dogs were playing with the ball now, knocking it back and forth. "Rachel, do you think Sunny could be one of the magic fairy pets?"

Rachel stared at the spaniel. He was standing with his head on one side, watching Bouncer, who'd picked up the ball and run off with it. "Yes, I think he might be," she agreed.

Meanwhile, Bouncer dropped the ball
to bark at Sunny. The ball landed on

the grassy slope and
began to roll down
the hill away
from the puppy,
gathering speed
all the time. It
was heading
straight towards
an open gate
which led out onto
the busy road beside
the showground. To the
girls' horror, Bouncer suddenly turned
and raced after it.

"Bouncer!" Rachel yelled in dismay,
as the puppy headed for the gate.
"Kirsty, we've got to stop him!"

With Sunny at their heels, the girls chased after the puppy, calling his name. But Bouncer was too intent on catching the ball to take any notice.

"We're too far away to catch him," Kirsty cried anxiously. "Bouncer, stop!"

But no sooner were the words out of Kirsty's mouth, than Sunny raced ahead of the girls and gave another little yap. Rachel blinked as she spotted a faint shimmer of silver fairy dust around Sunny, and the next moment, a big, meaty bone appeared in Bouncer's path.

The puppy skidded to a halt, ignoring
the ball as it bounced out of the gate
and onto the road; he was far more
interested in the juicy bone. With
a little yelp of delight, he lay down
to have a good chew.

"That was close!" Kirsty panted,
catching up and bending down to clip
Bouncer firmly to his lead again.

"Yes, that bone turned up just in time," Rachel agreed, patting Sunny. "You know, Kirsty, I think Bouncer suddenly slipping his lead, and then the ball and the bone appearing out of nowhere, can only mean one thing..."

Kirsty nodded seriously. "Sunny must be Lauren the Puppy Fairy's missing pet!" she declared.

Trouble Scoots Up

"He is!" laughed a light, silvery voice above the girls' heads.

Rachel and Kirsty glanced up. A pink balloon was floating down towards them, and holding onto the string, waving and smiling at them, was Lauren the Puppy Fairy.

"Hello," Kirsty and Rachel called, beaming happily. Sunny had spotted his owner too and was bouncing around excitedly.

Lauren floated down towards them, her long, light brown hair trailing in the breeze. She wore pink cargo pants embroidered with flowers on the pockets, a cropped pink top and trainers. Waving her wand at the girls, she fluttered down to stand on Sunny's back.

"I'm so glad to see you, Sunny!" Lauren cried happily, dropping a tiny kiss on top of her pet's head. "And you too, girls."

"We're pleased to see you as well," Kirsty replied.

"And I think Sunny's tail is going to drop off if he doesn't stop wagging it so hard!" Rachel laughed.

The spaniel gave a happy bark, turning his shaggy head to look lovingly at his owner as she petted him. Wondering what was going on, Bouncer looked up from his bone and trotted over to join them. He sniffed curiously at Lauren, and she put out her little hand to stroke his nose gently.

"I knew Sunny was around here somewhere," Lauren told the girls. "How clever of you to find him!"

Rachel and Kirsty smiled.

"Actually, he found us!" Rachel said.

"Well, he found Bouncer," put in Kirsty. "We've been lucky today though. We haven't seen any goblins!"

"Yes, this was the easiest pet

 rescue so far," Rachel agreed.

"Ha ha ha!" The sound of evil giggling behind them made Kirsty, Rachel, Lauren and even the puppies jump. Goblins!

A shiny silver scooter was speeding along the path towards them, and it was crowded with goblins. Two of them were using their feet to propel the scooter along as fast as they could. Meanwhile, three others were balanced on their shoulders, wobbling this way and that as the scooter zoomed along.

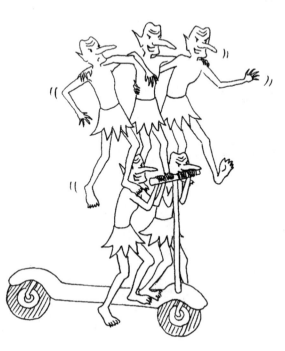

The girls and Lauren were taken by surprise. Before they could do anything, the scooter had crashed to a halt in front of them. The goblins tumbled off in an untidy heap. One rolled towards Sunny, and another towards Bouncer.

"Oof!" Lauren gasped, as the first goblin pushed her off Sunny's back, and then snatched up the puppy.

"Is this the magic puppy?" the goblin yelled to the others.

"Don't know!" they shouted back, looking from Sunny to Bouncer.

"Grab both!"

The first goblin leapt back on board the scooter, still clutching Sunny.

"Put him down!" Lauren yelled angrily, scrambling to her feet.

"Give him back!" shouted Rachel furiously, as the second goblin grabbed Bouncer, yanking the lead from Kirsty's hand, and then jumped onto the scooter.

"Catch us if you can!" jeered the
goblins, whizzing away down the hill,
twice as fast as they came up. The girls
and Lauren watched in outrage as the
scooter sped off, with both puppies
whimpering in fear.

"Jack Frost's going to be very pleased with us when he sees the magic puppy," one of the goblins shouted.

"Hurrah!" cheered his goblin friends.

Grabbed by Goblins!

"We must go after them!" Lauren declared, her face pale. "It'll be quicker if I turn you into fairies, girls."

Kirsty and Rachel nodded. Hearts thumping anxiously, they waited as Lauren waved her wand and showered them with sparkling pink fairy dust. As soon as they were fairy-sized, the girls fluttered up into the air to join their friend, and they all gave chase. But the goblins had a head start, and were whizzing further and further away.

"They're getting away!" Rachel gasped.

The goblins were heading in the direction of the bouncy castle. Rachel, Kirsty and Lauren could see that all the children had been cleared off the castle, and it was now slowly being deflated. Meanwhile, one of the goblins had climbed up onto the handlebars and was yelling instructions at the others.

"Turn left! No, not that way, you idiots!" he roared furiously.

The other goblins weren't taking any notice. They were struggling to hold the wriggling puppies, and arguing loudly at the same time.

"Not that way – this way!"

"No, that's not right!"

One of the goblins grabbed the handlebars and tried to yank them in the opposite direction. The goblin who was perched there almost fell off. But still the scooter zoomed down the hill, pulling even further away from Lauren, Rachel and Kirsty.

"Faster, girls!" Lauren called anxiously. "We must stop them!"

Kirsty frowned. The goblins were so far ahead, it seemed almost impossible to catch up with them. Her gaze fell on the slowly deflating bouncy castle, and that gave her an idea…

"Lauren!" Kirsty cried breathlessly. "Bouncer and Sunny are only puppies, but the goblins are scared of big dogs, aren't  they? I remember they were scared of Buttons, Rachel's dog."

Lauren nodded.

"Well, could you make a really big dog appear in front of the scooter?"

Kirsty went on. "Maybe we can make the goblins swerve and crash into the bouncy castle – that would slow them down."

"Great idea, Kirsty!" Rachel said eagerly. Lauren was already lifting her wand.

As the girls watched, a shower of pink, glittery sparkles whooshed from the tip of Lauren's wand towards the goblins. There was a puff of pink smoke, and then, just to the left of the scooter, an Alsatian appeared out of thin air. Rachel and Kirsty stared at it in surprise, because this was no ordinary Alsatian. It was black with white stripes, just like a zebra!

"Woof! Woof! Woof!" the dog barked loudly.

The goblins screeched with fright.

"A big, scary dog!" the one sitting
on the handlebars yelled. "Quick,
get away!"

All the goblins grabbed the handlebars
and wrenched them to the right.
Immediately, the scooter careened away
from the dog, straight towards the
bouncy castle.

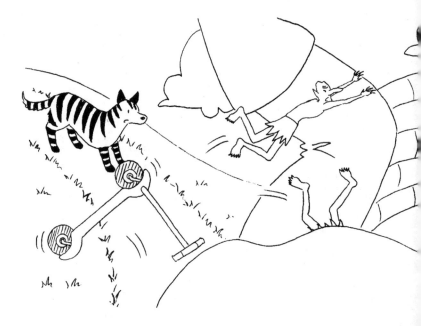

"No!" shouted the one on the handlebars. "We're going to crash!"

But he was too late. As Lauren, Rachel and Kirsty watched, the scooter hit the bouncy castle, sending the goblins flying. The puppies barked and the goblins shrieked with rage, but they all landed safely on the castle, disappearing into its billowing folds.

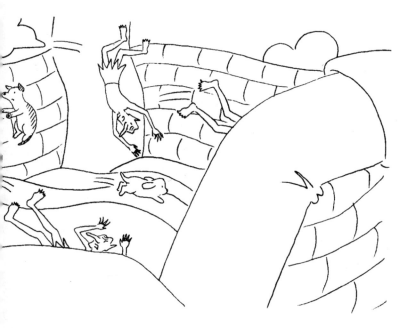

Quickly, Lauren waved her wand to make the Alsatian disappear and then she, Rachel and Kirsty flew over to the bouncy castle.

"It's a good thing there's hardly anyone around!" Kirsty said, looking very relieved.

"Yes, but what about the man who's packing the bouncy castle away?" Rachel asked anxiously. "He's sure to come back soon. How are we going to get the puppies and the goblins out of there?"

New Friends

Lauren, Kirsty and Rachel hovered over the bouncy castle, wondering what to do. But, to their relief, they suddenly heard a tiny bark.

A moment later Sunny's head popped out. He wriggled out of the castle, barking with delight as he spotted Lauren. Bouncer followed him, and together they bounced towards the edge of the half-deflated castle, clearly enjoying this new game.

"Sunny!" Lauren called, holding her arms open.

Rachel and Kirsty saw a shimmer of glittering magic around the spaniel as he shrank to fairy pet size. Then he jumped off the bouncy castle to bound magically through the air towards Lauren.

"It's OK, Bouncer," laughed Rachel, seeing the puppy staring at his doggy friend in surprise. "It's fairy magic!"

"Don't you try it, though!" Kirsty added with a laugh.

Sunny had run straight into Lauren's arms, and was now licking her nose gently. Laughing, Lauren raised her wand and in three sparkling seconds, Rachel and Kirsty were back to their normal size.

Bouncer blinked. Then he jumped down from the castle onto the ground and dashed joyfully over to Rachel and Kirsty. Rachel picked up his lead and held it firmly, as she bent down to pet him.

"What's Bouncer looking at?" asked Kirsty, noticing that the little puppy was staring curiously at something behind them.

Rachel turned to see. "Here comes the bouncy castle man!" she whispered. "Lauren – you and Sunny had better hide!"

Lauren nodded, and, still holding Sunny, she zoomed down to hide in Rachel's pocket.

The bouncy castle operator was a young man with a friendly face. He smiled at Kirsty and Rachel. "Hi," he said, "Did you enjoy the Spring show?"

"It was great," Kirsty replied, and Rachel nodded.

The man glanced down at Bouncer who was sniffing eagerly at his legs.

"What a lovely pup!" he said, bending down to scratch Bouncer's head. "My daughter, Annie, would love a dog like this."

"How old is Annie?" asked Rachel.

"She'll be six next week," the man replied, giving Bouncer another pat. "Actually, her mum and I are planning on getting her a puppy for her

 birthday. Excuse me," he went on, "I must get this castle put away." Whistling to himself, the man went off round the back of the bouncy castle, where all the cables and the electric blower were hidden.

"What are we going to do?" Rachel whispered anxiously, as Lauren and Sunny popped their heads out of her pocket. "He's not going to be very pleased when he finds a bunch of angry goblins in his castle."

But Kirsty was shaking her head and laughing. "Look!" She pointed at the front of the castle. "He won't see them because they're coming out this side. And it's the goblins who don't look very pleased!"

The goblins were finally emerging from beneath the folds of rubber. They were grumbling and groaning and blaming each other as usual. Two of them were dragging the silver scooter along. Complaining loudly, they all jumped to the ground and stalked off, pulling the scooter behind them.

"That was all your fault!"

"I told you we were going to crash!"

"And now we've lost the magic puppy. Who's going to tell Jack Frost?"

Kirsty, Rachel and Lauren couldn't help laughing.

"Daddy! Daddy, where are you?" came a voice.

Immediately, Lauren ducked out of sight and the girls turned to see who was coming.

A girl with dark curly hair and big blue eyes was running towards them. "Daddy, where are you?" she called again.

"Round the back of the castle, sweetheart," the man yelled back.

"That must be Annie," Kirsty whispered.

Just then, Annie caught sight of Bouncer. Her face broke into a huge smile and she dashed straight towards him. "What a gorgeous puppy!" she said, kneeling down to hug him. Bouncer yapped a greeting and licked her cheek, his tail wagging furiously.

"Oh, I wish I had a puppy like him!"

"Would you like to hold his lead?"
Rachel asked, offering it to her.

Annie's eyes lit up.
"Can I really?"
she gasped.
"Oh, thank you!"

She took the
lead, and Kirsty
and Rachel
watched as she
took Bouncer
on a little walk
up and down
in front of the
castle. Bouncer
bounded alongside
her, obviously
enjoying himself.

63

Then he spied the trailing lace of one of Annie's trainers, and pounced on it, grabbing it in his teeth.

Annie laughed and crouched down to tug the lace gently. Kirsty and Rachel smiled as Bouncer held on to it, enjoying the game.

Suddenly, Kirsty nudged Rachel. "Look, Rachel!" she whispered, her voice full of excitement. "There's a magical sparkle all around Annie and Bouncer!"

Puppy Love

Rachel stared at the little girl and the puppy. Kirsty was right! A slight, shimmery haze hung in the air around them.

"Fairy magic!" Rachel whispered back. "Bouncer's meant to be with Annie. She's the owner he's been waiting for!"

At that moment the man came out from behind the bouncy castle, which was now almost fully deflated. He smiled as he saw Annie and Bouncer playing together.

"He really is a lovely puppy, girls,"

he said with a smile. "Which one of you does he belong to?"

Rachel saw her chance. "He's not mine or Kirsty's," she explained. "He's from the animal shelter stall. His brothers and sisters have been adopted today, and he's the only one left."

"Oh, really?" The man frowned. "I didn't see the animal shelter stall."

Annie had been listening
to their conversation, her
eyes wide. Now she
tugged at her dad's
sleeve. "Daddy!"
she cried. "This
poor little puppy
hasn't got a home!"

Rachel and Kirsty
held their breath as they
waited for Annie's dad to reply. He
looked at the eager face of his little
girl, and then down into Bouncer's
brown eyes.

"Well..." he began, "I'll finish up
here, and then we'll go over to the
animal shelter stall. But don't get your
hopes up too much, Annie. Someone
else may want to adopt him."

"Oh, thank you, Daddy!" Annie gasped joyfully, throwing her arms around him. Rachel and Kirsty beamed at each other. Even Bouncer seemed to know that something exciting was going on, because he gave two happy barks.

The man disappeared behind the castle to finish off, and Annie and Bouncer went with him.

"Well done, girls!" Lauren said, flying out of Rachel's pocket. Sunny followed her, bounding through the air to perch on Kirsty's shoulder. "Annie is the puppy's perfect owner!"

"Everything's worked out brilliantly," Rachel said happily, and Kirsty nodded.

"I don't know how I can ever thank you," Lauren went on gratefully. "Without you, I wouldn't have got my darling Sunny back."

"Woof!" Sunny agreed, rubbing his tiny black nose against Kirsty's cheek.

"But we must go home to Fairyland now," Lauren said, raising her wand. "Everyone will be anxious to find out if I've got my magic pet back. Say goodbye, Sunny."

Sunny gave a little yap, wagging his tail so hard it tickled Kirsty's ear. Then he ran over to Lauren, who waved her wand so that a shower of sparkling fairy dust fell around them.

"Oh!" Lauren called, "I nearly forgot! Say goodbye to Barney for me, won't you?"

Puzzled, Rachel and Kirsty looked at each other.

"Who's Barney?" asked Rachel. But Lauren and Sunny had vanished in a haze of glittering magic.

A moment later, Annie, Bouncer and her dad appeared.

"Daddy, we'll have to give my new puppy a name," Annie was saying. "Can I call him Barney?"

Her dad smiled. "We must talk to the people at the animal shelter before we make any plans," he said. "But if it's OK for us to adopt him, then we'll call him Barney."

Rachel and Kirsty grinned at each other, as they followed Annie and her father towards the animal shelter stall.

"So that's why Lauren told us to say goodbye to Barney!" Kirsty whispered. "Mr Gregory's going to be really pleased that Barney's found a home at last."

The two girls beamed as they watched Annie's father chatting to Mr Gregory. The vet was nodding and smiling, and Annie and Barney were chasing each other up and down.

"Everyone in Fairyland's going to be pleased that Sunny's safely home again, too!" Rachel added happily.

Kirsty nodded. "I love happy endings!" she sighed.

RAINBOW magic ®

The Pet Keeper Fairies

Lauren the Puppy Fairy has got her
pet back. Now Rachel and Kirsty
must help

Harriet the Hamster Fairy

Win a Rainbow Magic
Sparkly T-Shirt and Goody Bag!

In every book in the Rainbow Magic Pet Keeper Fairies series (books 29-35) there is a hidden picture of a collar with a secret letter in it. Find all seven letters and re-arrange them to make a special Fairyland word, then send it to us. Each month we will put the entries into a draw and select one winner to receive a Rainbow Magic Sparkly T-shirt and Goody Bag!

Send your entry on a postcard to Rainbow Magic Pet Keeper Competition, Orchard Books, 338 Euston Road, London NW1 3BH. Australian readers should write to Hachette Children's Books, Level 17/207 Kent Street, Sydney, NSW 2000.
Don't forget to include your name and address.
Only one entry per child. Final draw: 30th April 2007.

Don't miss...
Kylie the Carnival Fairy

1-84616-175-4

Kylie the Carnival Fairy needs Kirsty's and Rachel's help! Jack Frost has stolen the three magic hats that make the Sunnydays Carnival so much fun, and the girls have to get them back...

Have you checked out the

website at:

www.rainbowmagic.co.uk

There are games, activities and fun things to do, as well as news and information about Rainbow Magic and all of the fairies.

by Daisy Meadows

The Rainbow Fairies

The Weather Fairies

The Party Fairies

The Jewel Fairies

India the Moonstone Fairy	ISBN	1 84362 958 5
Scarlett the Garnet Fairy	ISBN	1 84362 954 2
Emily the Emerald Fairy	ISBN	1 84362 955 0
Chloe the Topaz Fairy	ISBN	1 84362 956 9
Amy the Amethyst Fairy	ISBN	1 84362 957 7
Sophie the Sapphire Fairy	ISBN	1 84362 953 4
Lucy the Diamond Fairy	ISBN	1 84362 959 3

The Pet Keeper Fairies

Katie the Kitten Fairy	ISBN	1 84616 166 5
Bella the Bunny Fairy	ISBN	1 84616 170 3
Georgia the Guinea Pig Fairy	ISBN	1 84616 168 1
Lauren the Puppy Fairy	ISBN	1 84616 169 X
Harriet the Hamster Fairy	ISBN	1 84616 167 3
Molly the Goldfish Fairy	ISBN	1 84616 172 X
Penny the Pony Fairy	ISBN	1 84616 171 1
Holly the Christmas Fairy	ISBN	1 84362 661 6
Summer the Holiday Fairy	ISBN	1 84362 960 7
Stella the Star Fairy	ISBN	1 84362 869 4
Kylie the Carnival Fairy	ISBN	1 84616 175 4
The Rainbow Magic Treasury	ISBN	1 84616 047 2

All priced at £3.99. *Holly the Christmas Fairy, Summer the Holiday Fairy, Stella the Star Fairy* and *Kylie the Carnival Fairy* are priced at £4.99.
The Rainbow Magic Treasury is priced at £12.99.
Rainbow Magic books are available from all good bookshops, or can be ordered direct from the publisher: Orchard Books, PO BOX 29, Douglas IM99 1BQ
Credit card orders please telephone 01624 836000
or fax 01624 837033 or visit our Internet site: www.wattspub.co.uk
or e-mail: bookshop@enterprise.net for details.

To order please quote title, author and ISBN and your full name and address.
Cheques and postal orders should be made payable to 'Bookpost plc.'
Postage and packing is FREE within the UK
(overseas customers should add £2.00 per book).
Prices and availability are subject to change.

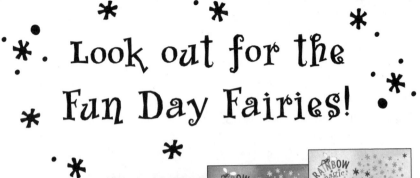

Look out for the Fun Day Fairies!

MEGAN THE MONDAY FAIRY
1-84616-188-6

TALLULAH THE TUESDAY FAIRY
1-84616-189-4

WILLOW THE WEDNESDAY FAIRY
1-84616-190-8

THEA THE THURSDAY FAIRY
1-84616-191-6

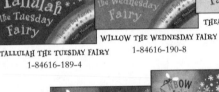

FREYA THE FRIDAY FAIRY
1-84616-192-4

SIENNA THE SATURDAY FAIRY
1-84616-193-2

SARAH THE SUNDAY FAIRY
1-84616-194-0

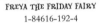

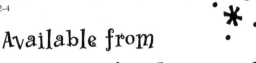

Available from
Saturday 2nd September 2006